Giggle, Giggle, Quack

For Andrew — D. C.
To Rosanne Lauer — B. L.

SIMON SPOTLIGHT
An imprint of Simon & Schuster Children's Publishing Division
1230 Avenue of the Americas, New York, New York 10020
This Simon Spotlight edition December 2016
Text copyright © 2000 by Doreen Cronin
Illustrations copyright © 2000 by Betsy Lewin
SIMON SPOTLIGHT, READY-TO-READ, and colophon are registered trademarks of Simon & Schuster, Inc.
For information about special discounts for bulk purchases, please contact Simon & Schuster Special Sales at
1-866-506-1949 or business@simonandschuster.com.
Manufactured in the United States of America 1116 LAK
2 4 6 8 10 9 7 5 3 1
Cataloging-in-Publication Data is available from the Library of Congress.
ISBN 978-1-4814-6544-1 (hc)
ISBN 978-1-4814-6543-4 (pbk)
ISBN 978-1-4814-6545-8 (eBook)

Giggle, Giggle, Quack

by Doreen Cronin   pictures by Betsy Lewin

Ready-to-Read

Simon Spotlight

New York   London   Toronto   Sydney   New Delhi

Farmer Brown was going
on vacation.
He left his brother, Bob, in charge
of the animals.

"I wrote everything down for you.
Just follow my instructions
and everything will be fine,"
said Farmer Brown.
"But keep an eye on Duck.
He's trouble."

Farmer Brown thought he heard
giggles and snickers
as he drove away,
but he couldn't be sure.

Bob gave Duck a good long stare
and went inside.
He read the first note:

Tuesday night
is pizza night
(not the frozen
kind!).
The hens prefer
anchovies.

Giggle, giggle, cluck.

Twenty-nine minutes later
there was hot pizza in the barn.

Bob checked on the animals before he went to bed. Everything was just fine.

Wednesday is bath day
for the pigs.
Wash them with my
favorite bubble bath and
dry them off with my
good towels.
Remember, they have
very sensitive skin.

Giggle, giggle, oink.

Bob had all the pigs washed
in no time.

Farmer Brown called home on Wednesday night to check in. "Did you feed the animals like I wrote in the note?" he asked.

"Done," replied Bob, counting seven empty pizza boxes.

"Did you see my note about the pigs?" asked Farmer Brown. "All taken care of," said Bob proudly. "Are you keeping a very close eye on Duck?" Farmer Brown asked. Bob gave Duck a good long stare. Duck was too busy sharpening his pencil to notice.

"Just keep him in the house,"
ordered Farmer Brown.
"He's a bad influence on the cows."

Giggle, giggle, moo, giggle, oink, giggle, quack.

Thursday night is movie night. It's the cows' turn to pick.

Giggle, giggle, moo.

Bob was in the kitchen, popping corn.
Just as the animals settled in
to watch THE SOUND OF MOOSIC,
the phone rang.

The only thing Farmer Brown heard on the other end was:

"Giggle, giggle, quack, giggle, moo, giggle, oink...."

UH-OH.

"DUCK!"

"DUCK!" screamed Farmer Brown.